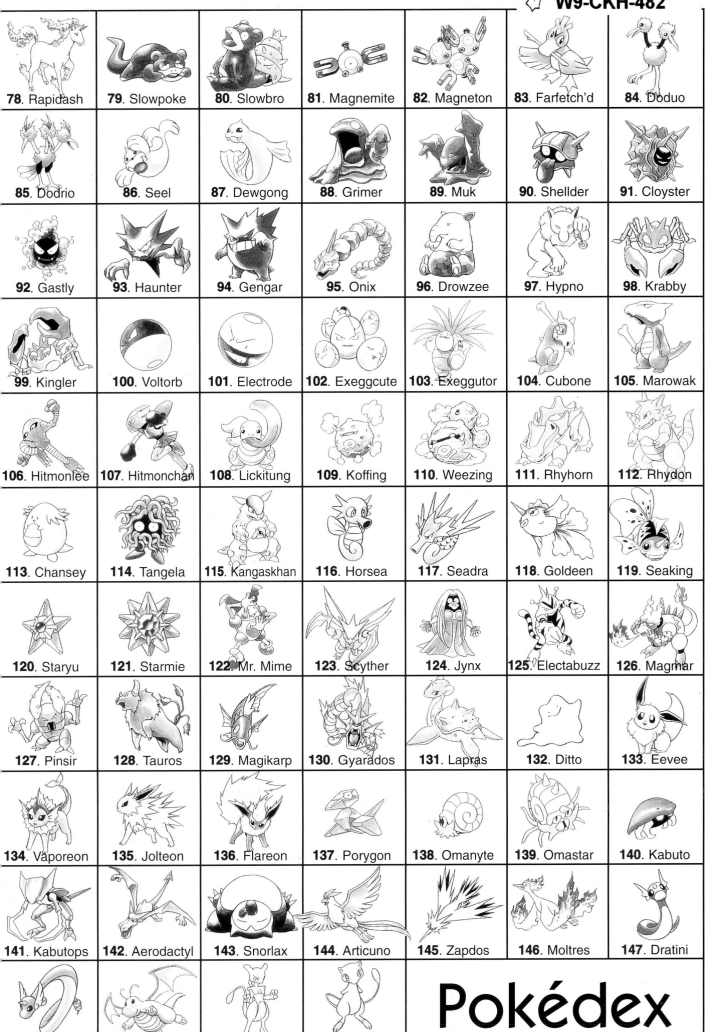

78. Rapidash	**79**. Slowpoke	**80**. Slowbro	**81**. Magnemite	**82**. Magneton	**83**. Farfetch'd	**84**. Doduo
85. Dodrio	**86**. Seel	**87**. Dewgong	**88**. Grimer	**89**. Muk	**90**. Shellder	**91**. Cloyster
92. Gastly	**93**. Haunter	**94**. Gengar	**95**. Onix	**96**. Drowzee	**97**. Hypno	**98**. Krabby
99. Kingler	**100**. Voltorb	**101**. Electrode	**102**. Exeggcute	**103**. Exeggutor	**104**. Cubone	**105**. Marowak
106. Hitmonlee	**107**. Hitmonchan	**108**. Lickitung	**109**. Koffing	**110**. Weezing	**111**. Rhyhorn	**112**. Rhydon
113. Chansey	**114**. Tangela	**115**. Kangaskhan	**116**. Horsea	**117**. Seadra	**118**. Goldeen	**119**. Seaking
120. Staryu	**121**. Starmie	**122**. Mr. Mime	**123**. Scyther	**124**. Jynx	**125**. Electabuzz	**126**. Magmar
127. Pinsir	**128**. Tauros	**129**. Magikarp	**130**. Gyarados	**131**. Lapras	**132**. Ditto	**133**. Eevee
134. Vaporeon	**135**. Jolteon	**136**. Flareon	**137**. Porygon	**138**. Omanyte	**139**. Omastar	**140**. Kabuto
141. Kabutops	**142**. Aerodactyl	**143**. Snorlax	**144**. Articuno	**145**. Zapdos	**146**. Moltres	**147**. Dratini
148. Dragonair	**149**. Dragonite	**150**. Mewtwo	**151**. Mew			

Pokédex

3

PALLET TOWN ON PARADE

LET'S FIND

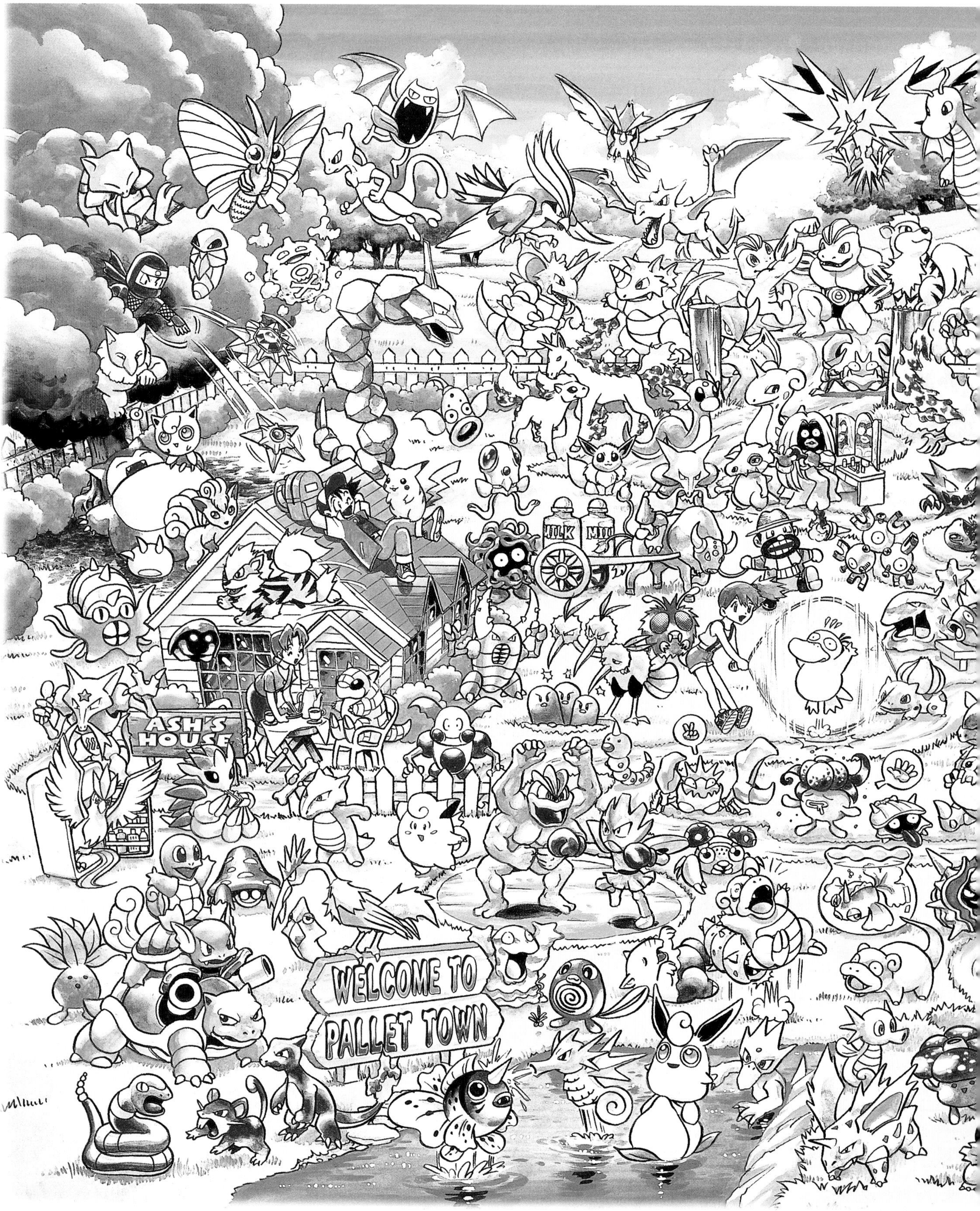

ASH'S HOUSE
MILK
WELCOME TO PALLET TOWN

POKéMON!

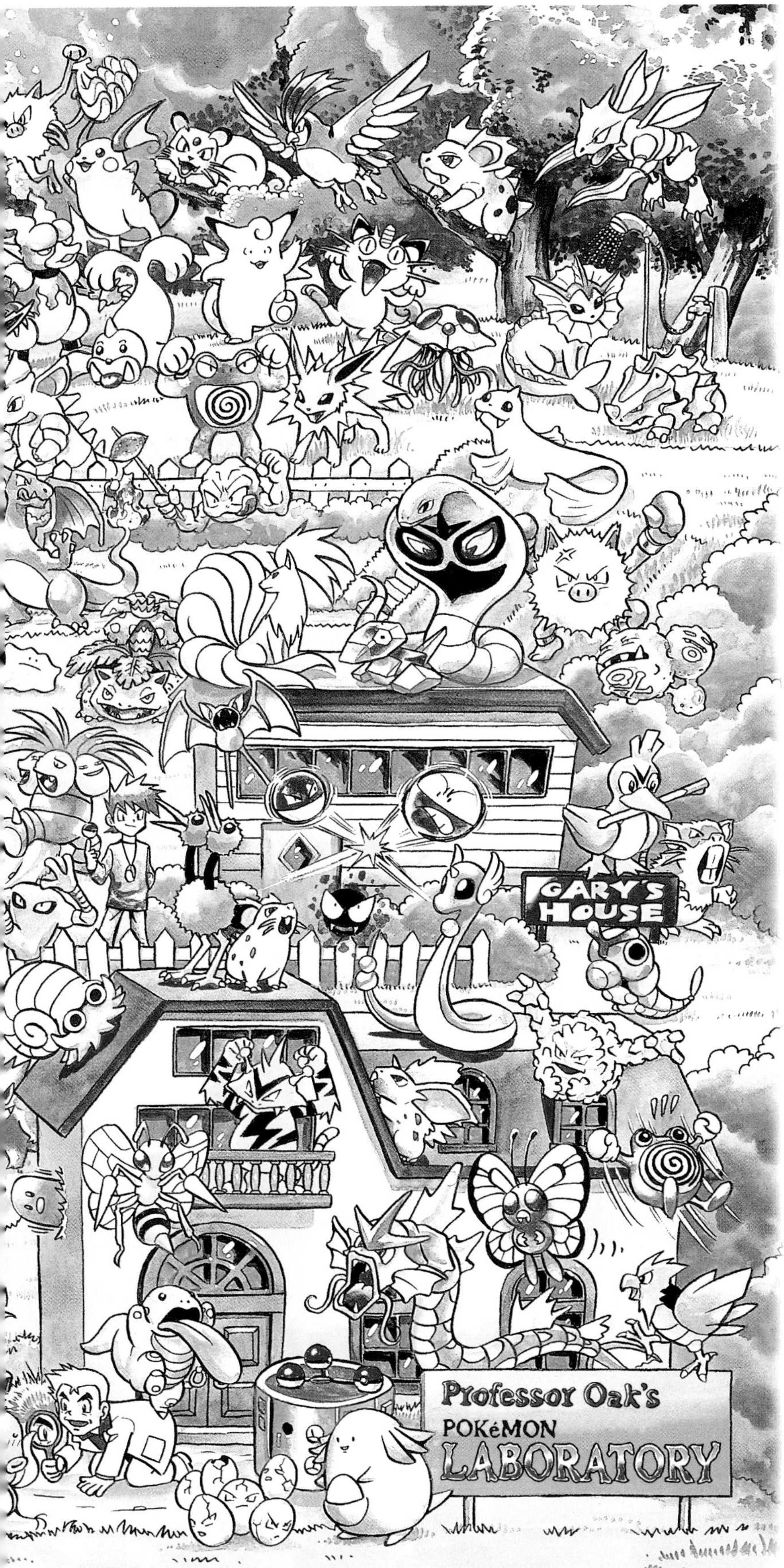
GARY'S HOUSE
Professor Oak's
POKéMON
LABORATORY

HOW TO HAVE FUN WITH THIS BOOK

1. Look at the pictures and find the hidden Pokémon.
2. If you give up, the answers are on page 20!
3. The page after that (page 21) has a list of other Pokémon that you will have to search through the whole book to find. (These are a little harder!)
4. Two Pokémon mini-stories are taking place from one picture to the next. You can learn about them on page 22.

Can you find the Pokémon?

Look for the 5 Pokémon pictured below!

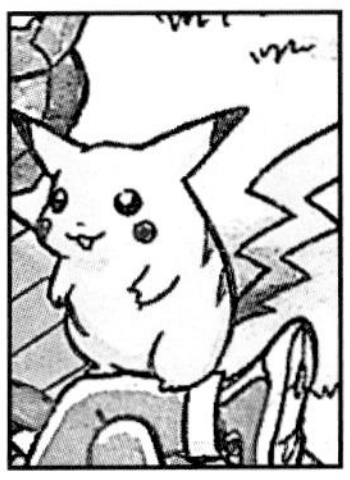
Pikachu

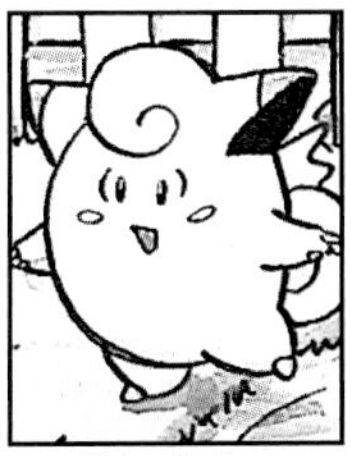
Clefairy

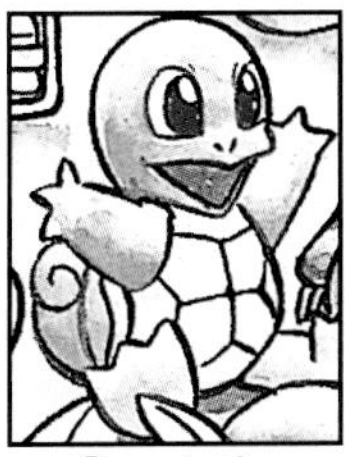
Squirtle

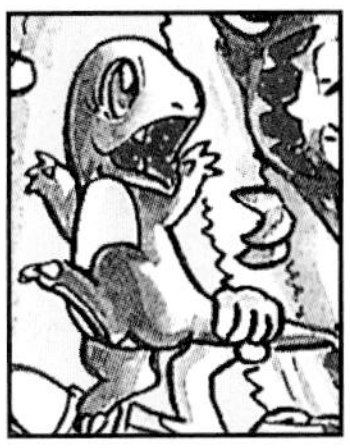
Charmander

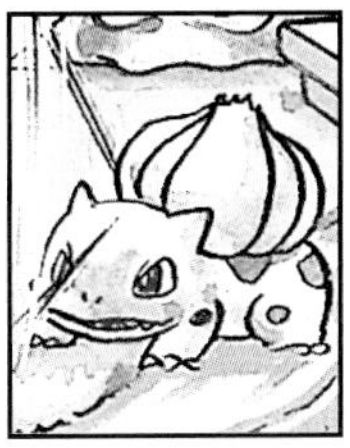
Bulbasaur

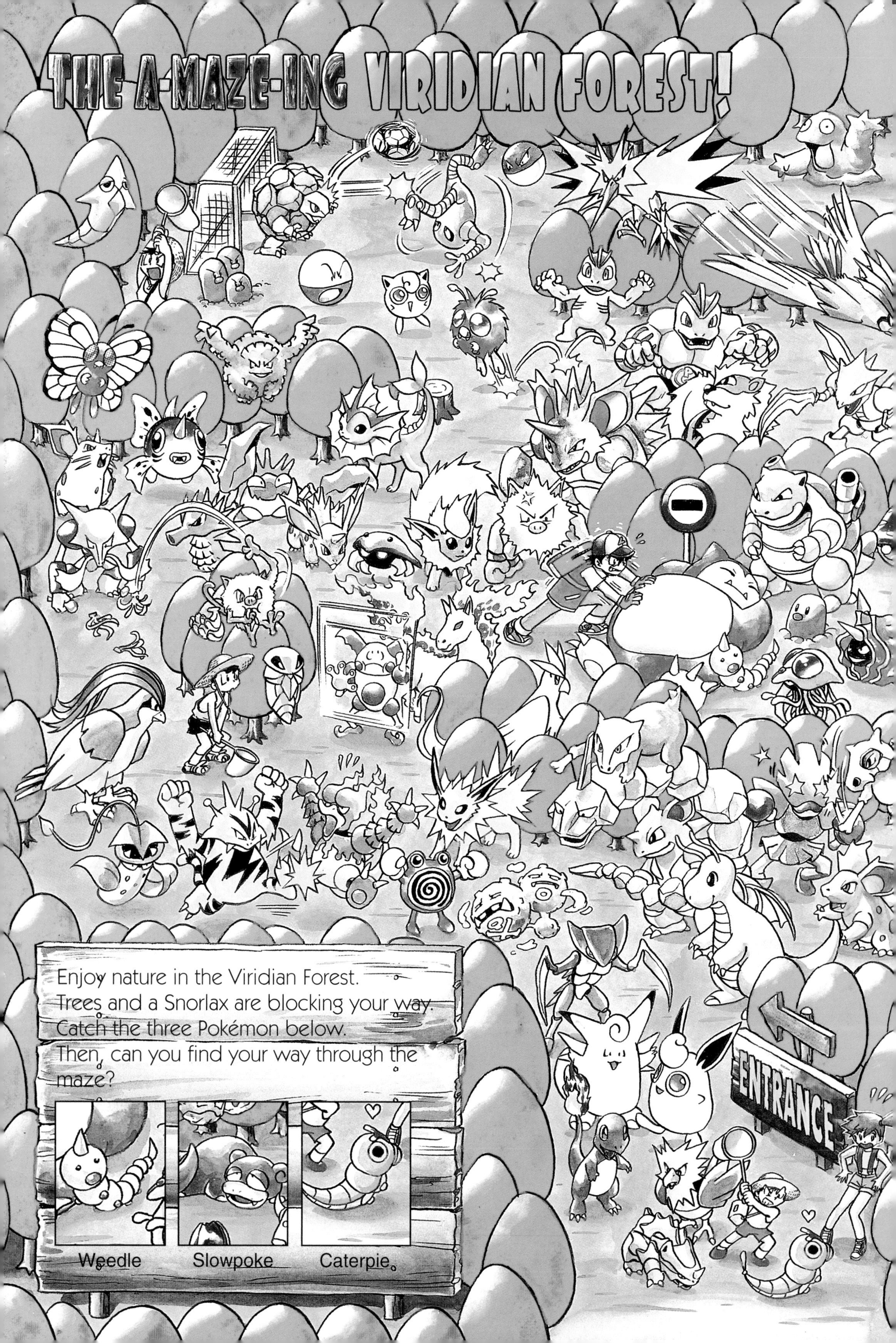
THE A-MAZE-ING VIRIDIAN FOREST!
Enjoy nature in the Viridian Forest.
Trees and a Snorlax are blocking your way.
Catch the three Pokémon below.
Then, can you find your way through the maze?
Weedle
Slowpoke
Caterpie
ENTRANCE

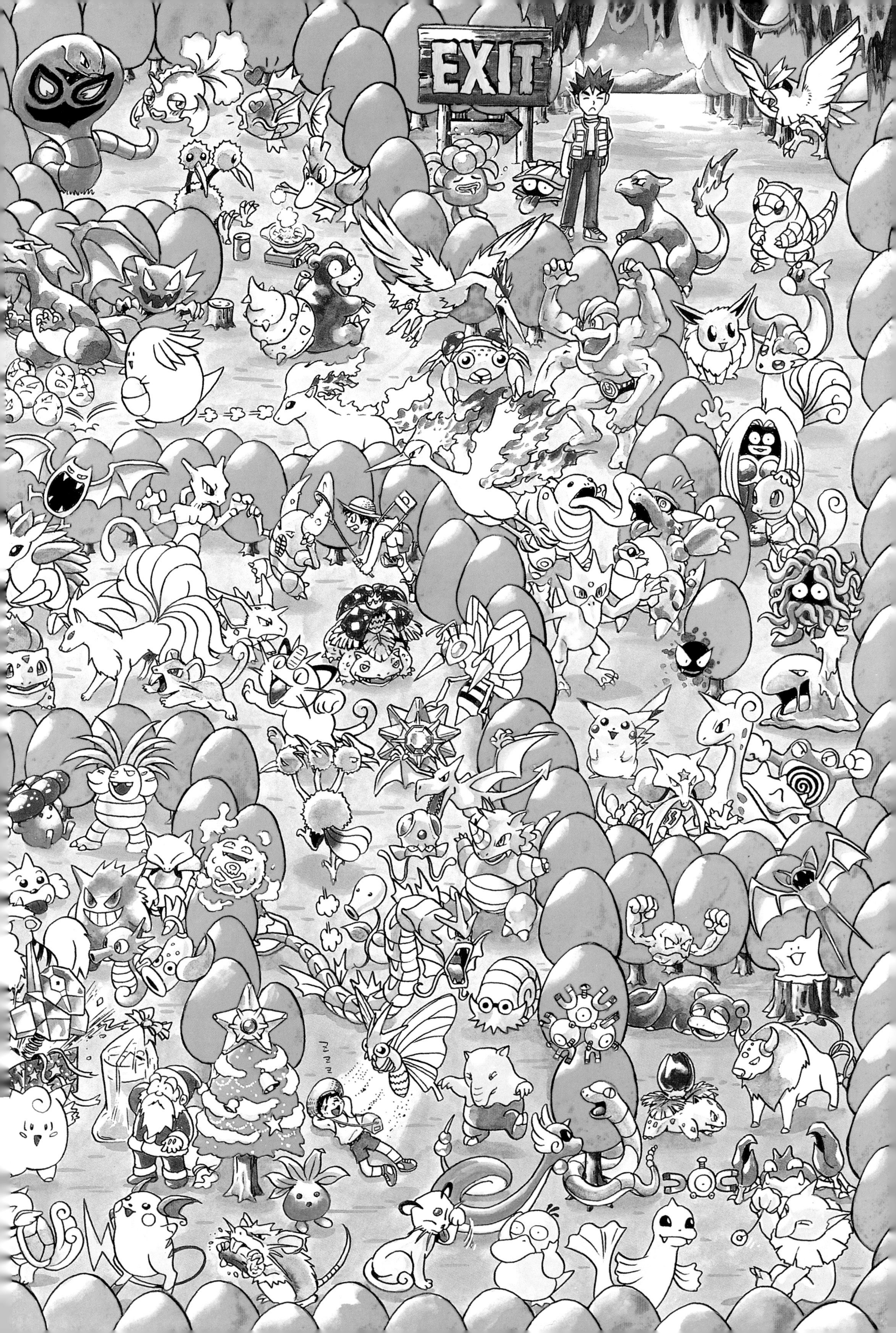
EXIT

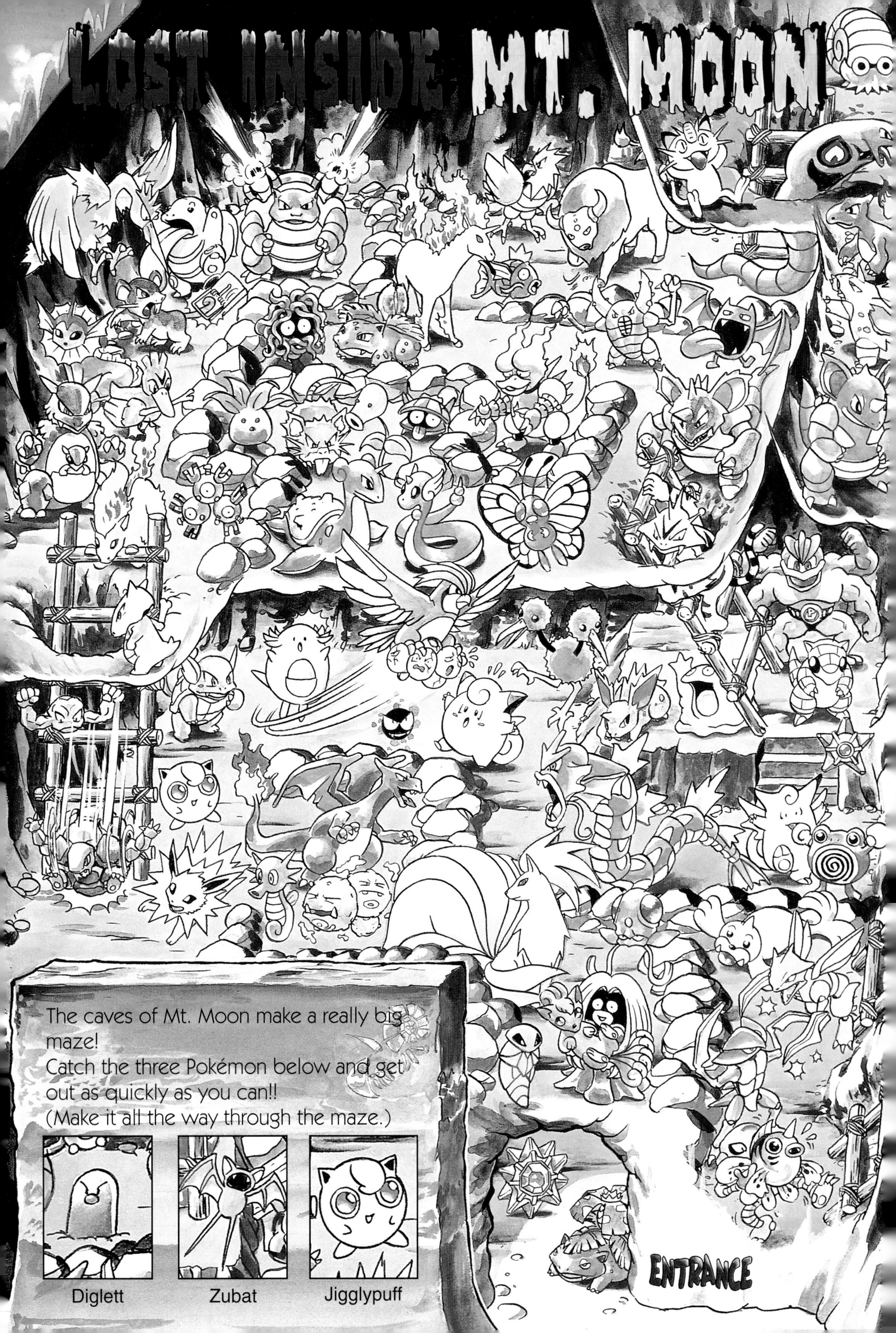
LOST INSIDE MT. MOON
The caves of Mt. Moon make a really big maze!
Catch the three Pokémon below and get out as quickly as you can!!
(Make it all the way through the maze.)
Diglett
Zubat
Jigglypuff
ENTRANCE

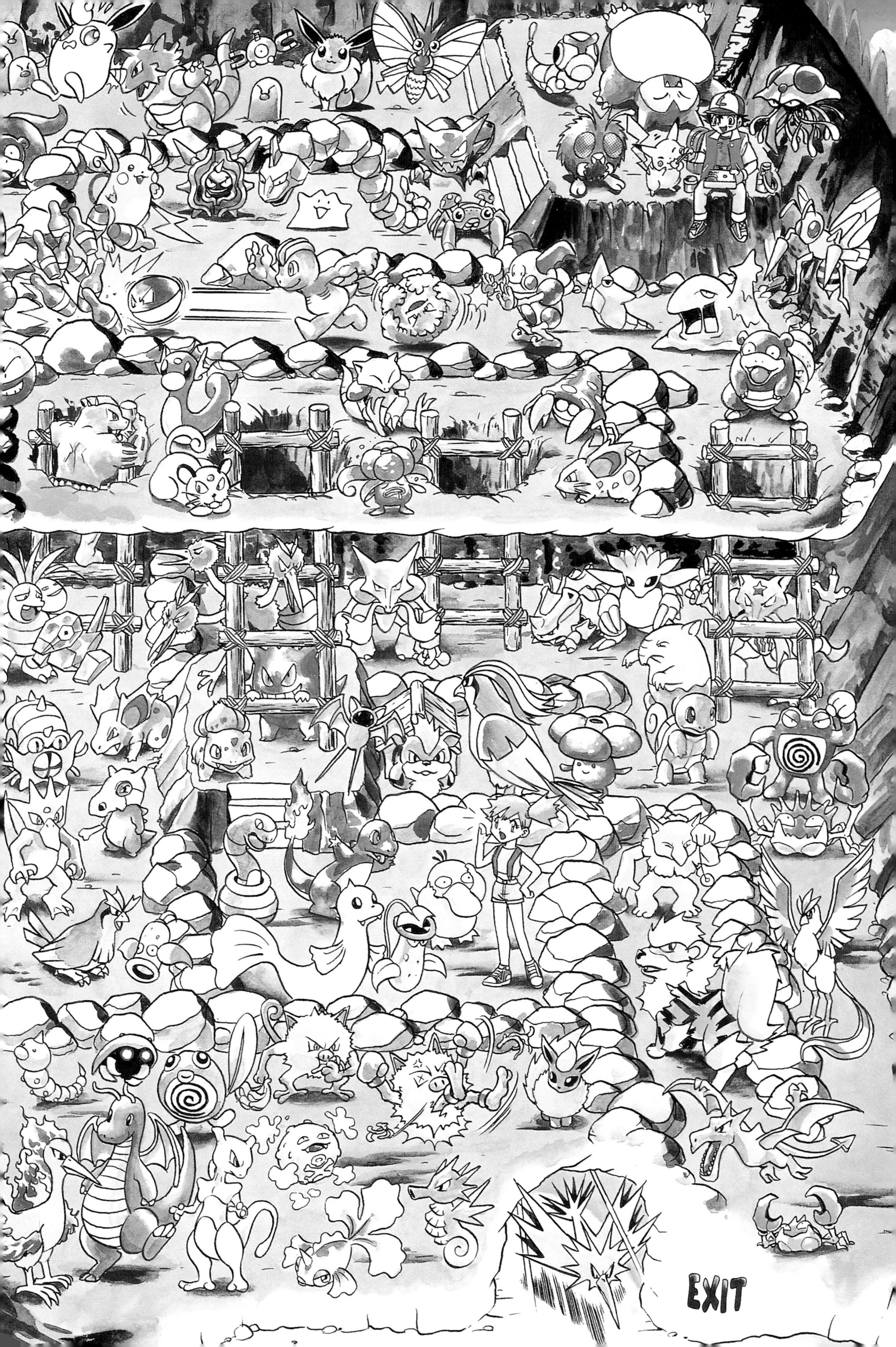
EXIT

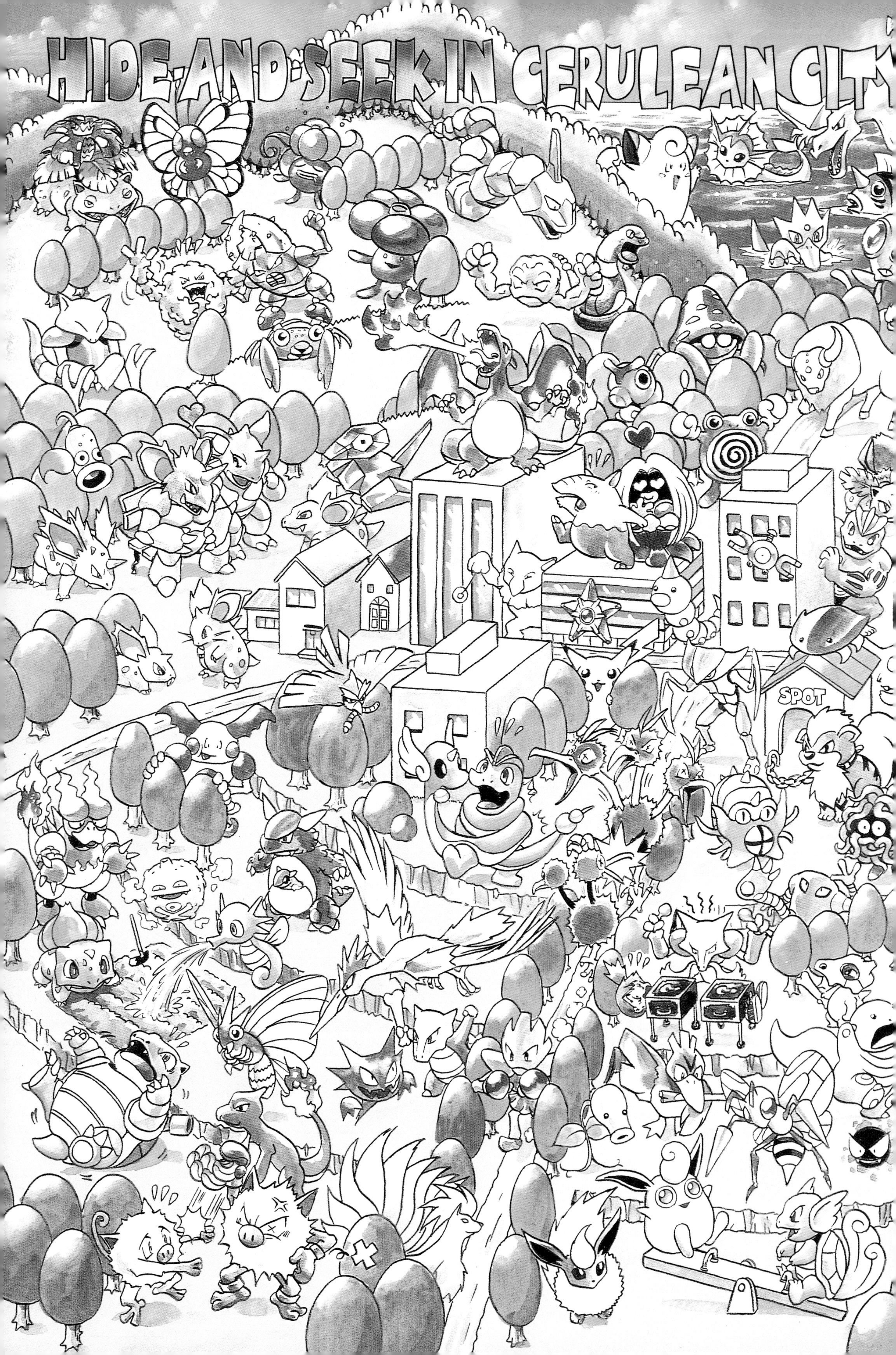
HIDE-AND-SEEK IN CERULEAN CITY
SPOT

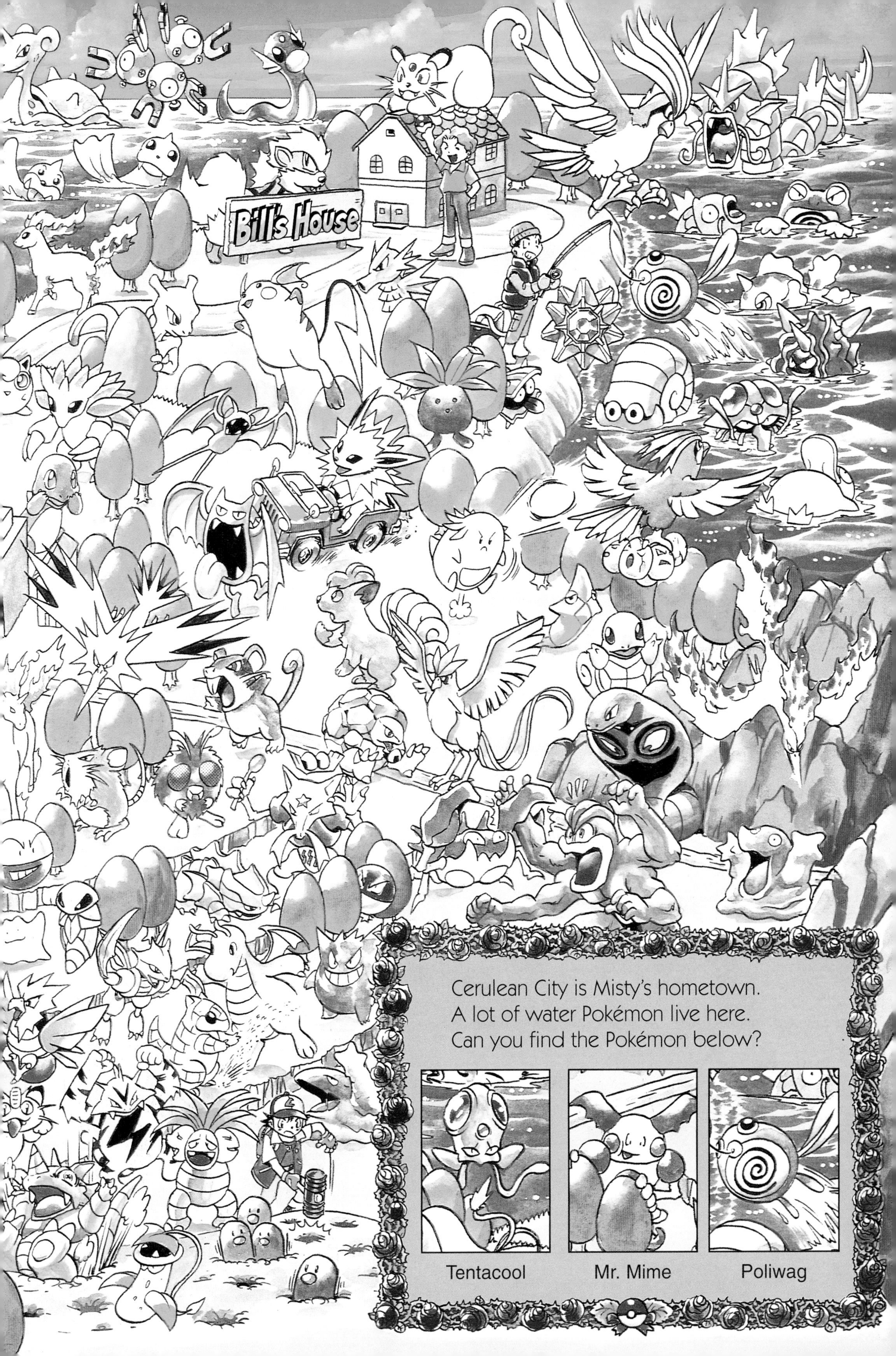
Bill's House
Cerulean City is Misty's hometown.
A lot of water Pokémon live here.
Can you find the Pokémon below?
Tentacool
Mr. Mime
Poliwag

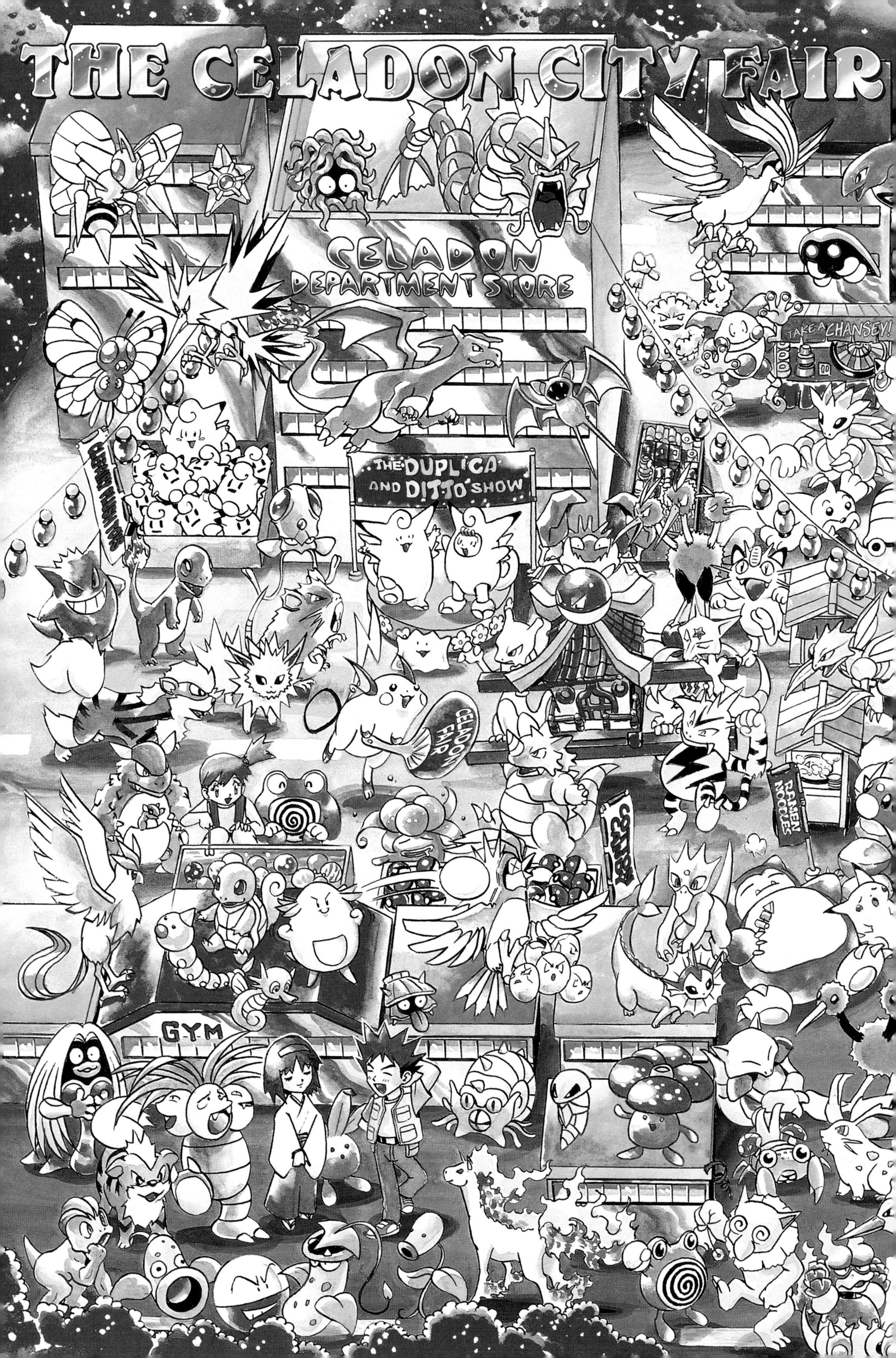
THE CELADON CITY FAIR
CELADON
DEPARTMENT STORE
TAKE A CHANSEY!
CLEFAIRY PLUSH TOYS
THE DUPLICA AND DITTO SHOW
CELADON FAIR
RAMEN NOODLES
COTTON CANDY
GYM

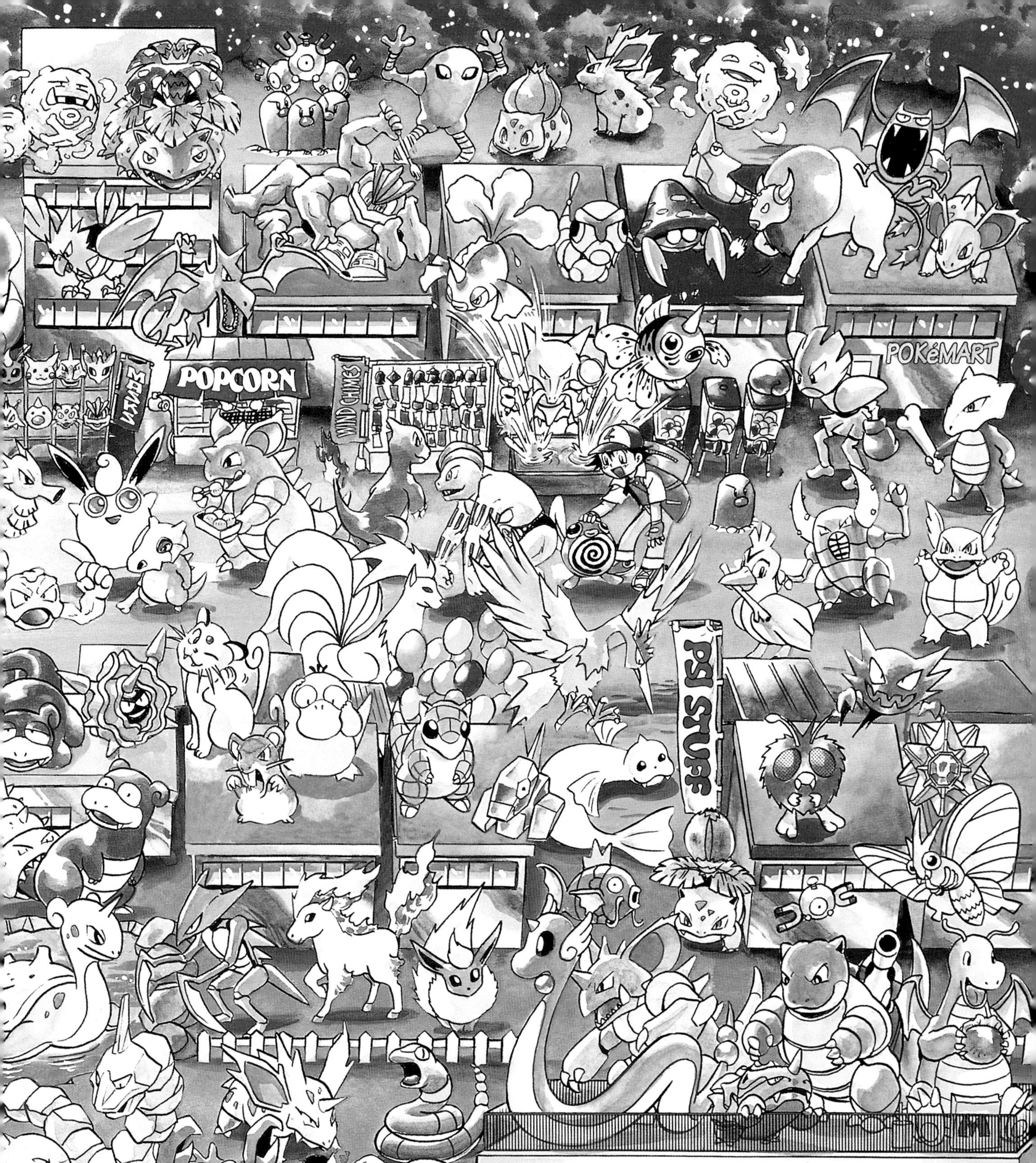
POPCORN
WIND CHIMES
PSI STUFF
POKéMART

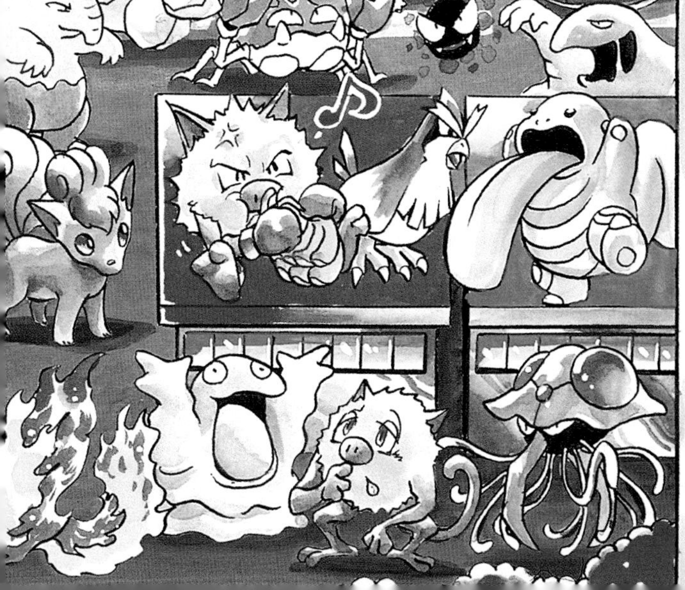

Celadon City is a big town.
Today is the day of the Celadon Fair! Go have fun!
All the Pokémon are here for the fair, too.
Have a great time, everybody!

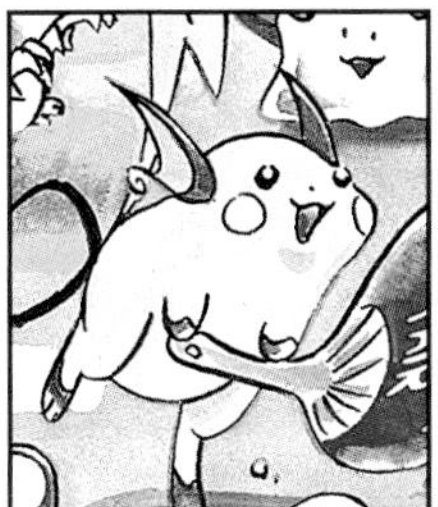

Raichu

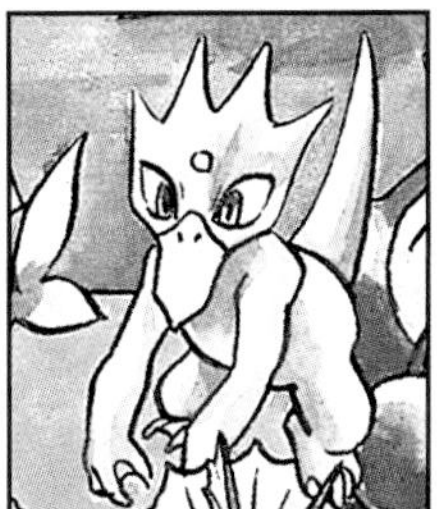

Golduck

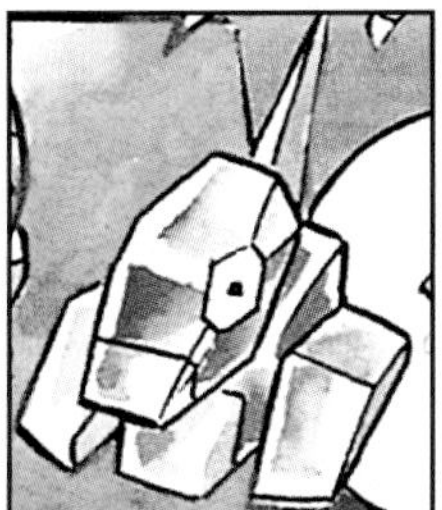

Porygon

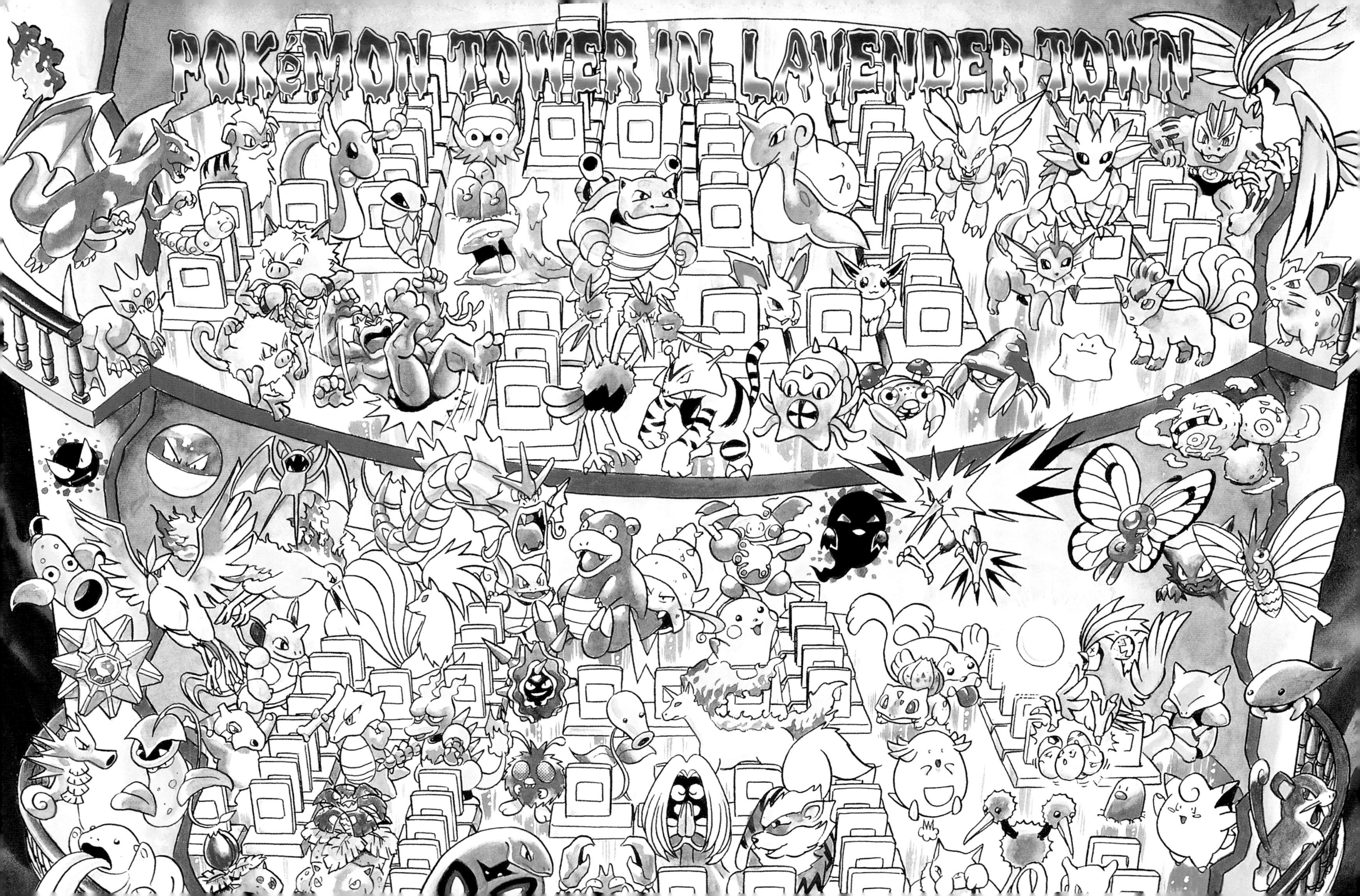
POKéMON TOWER IN LAVENDER TOWN

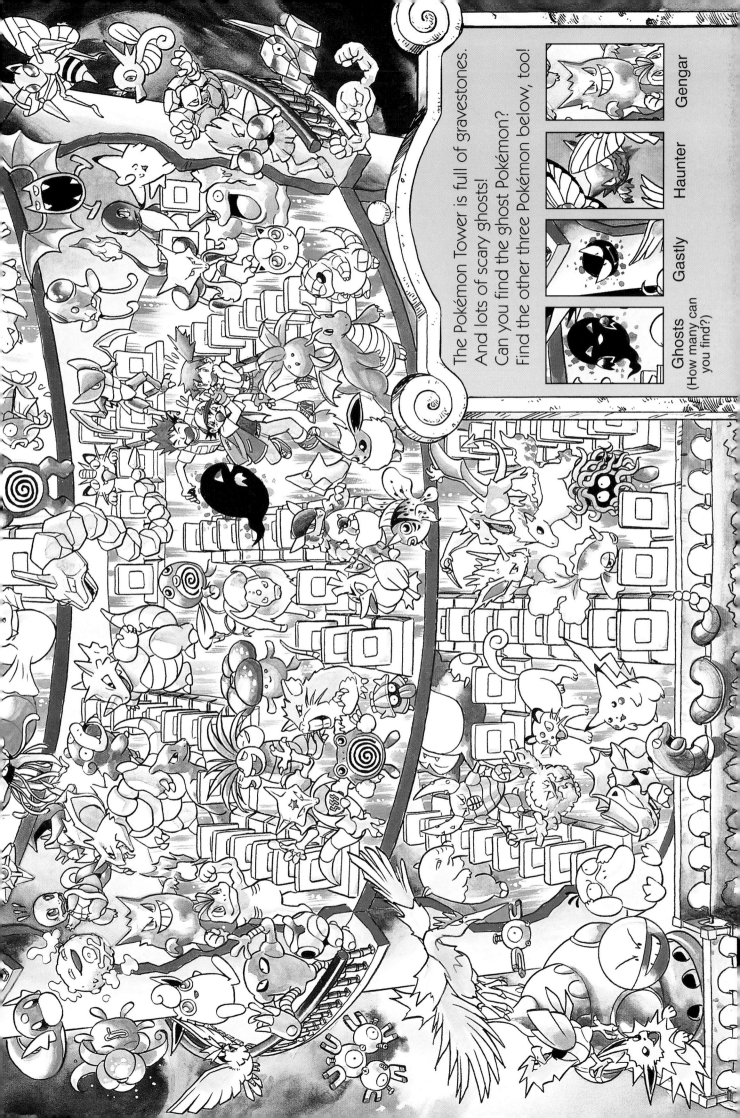

The Pokémon Tower is full of gravestones.
And lots of scary ghosts!
Can you find the ghost Pokémon?
Find the other three Pokémon below, too!

Ghosts
(How many can you find?)

Gastly

Haunter

Gengar

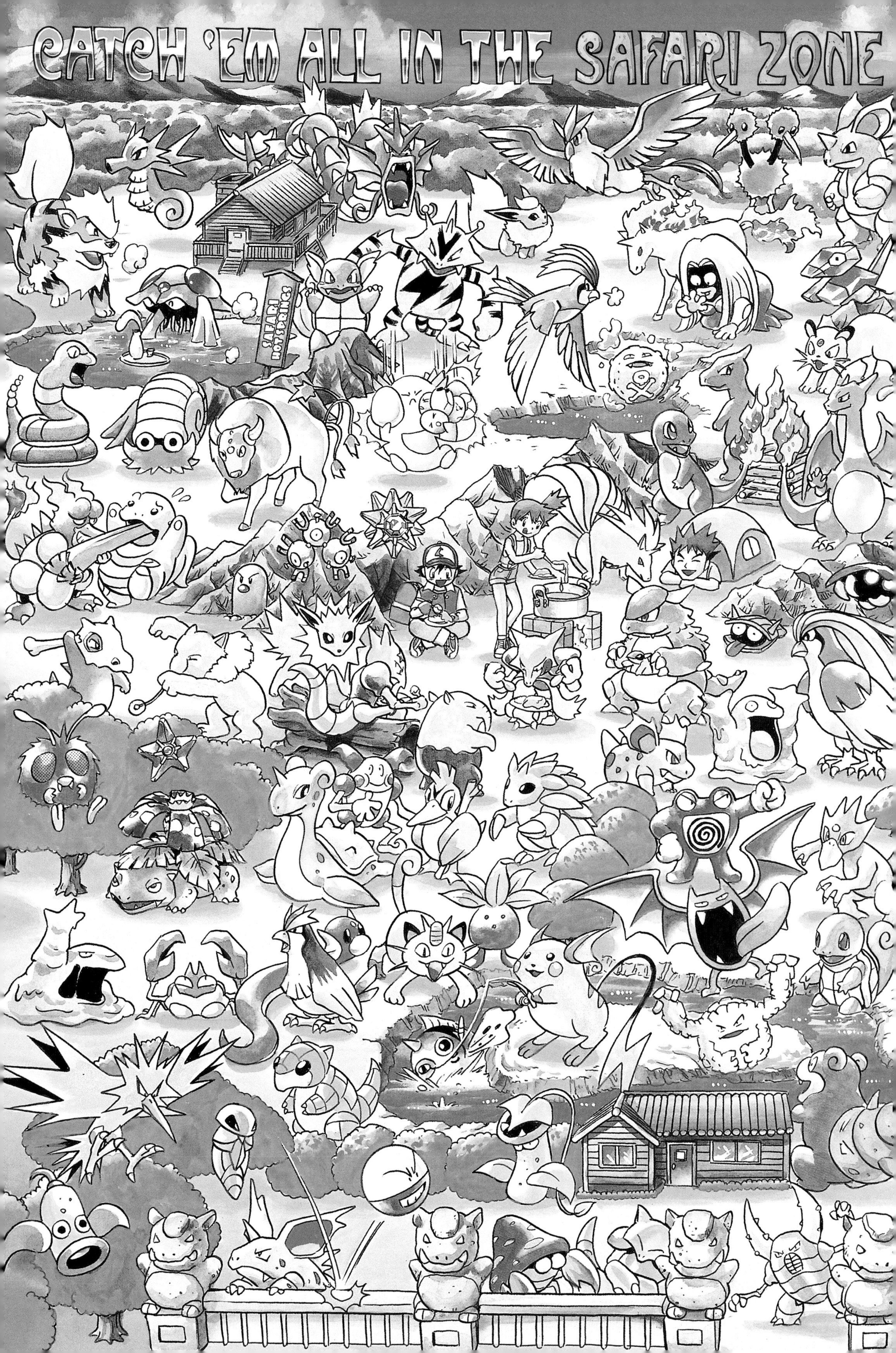
CATCH 'EM ALL IN THE SAFARI ZONE
SAFARI HOT SPRINGS

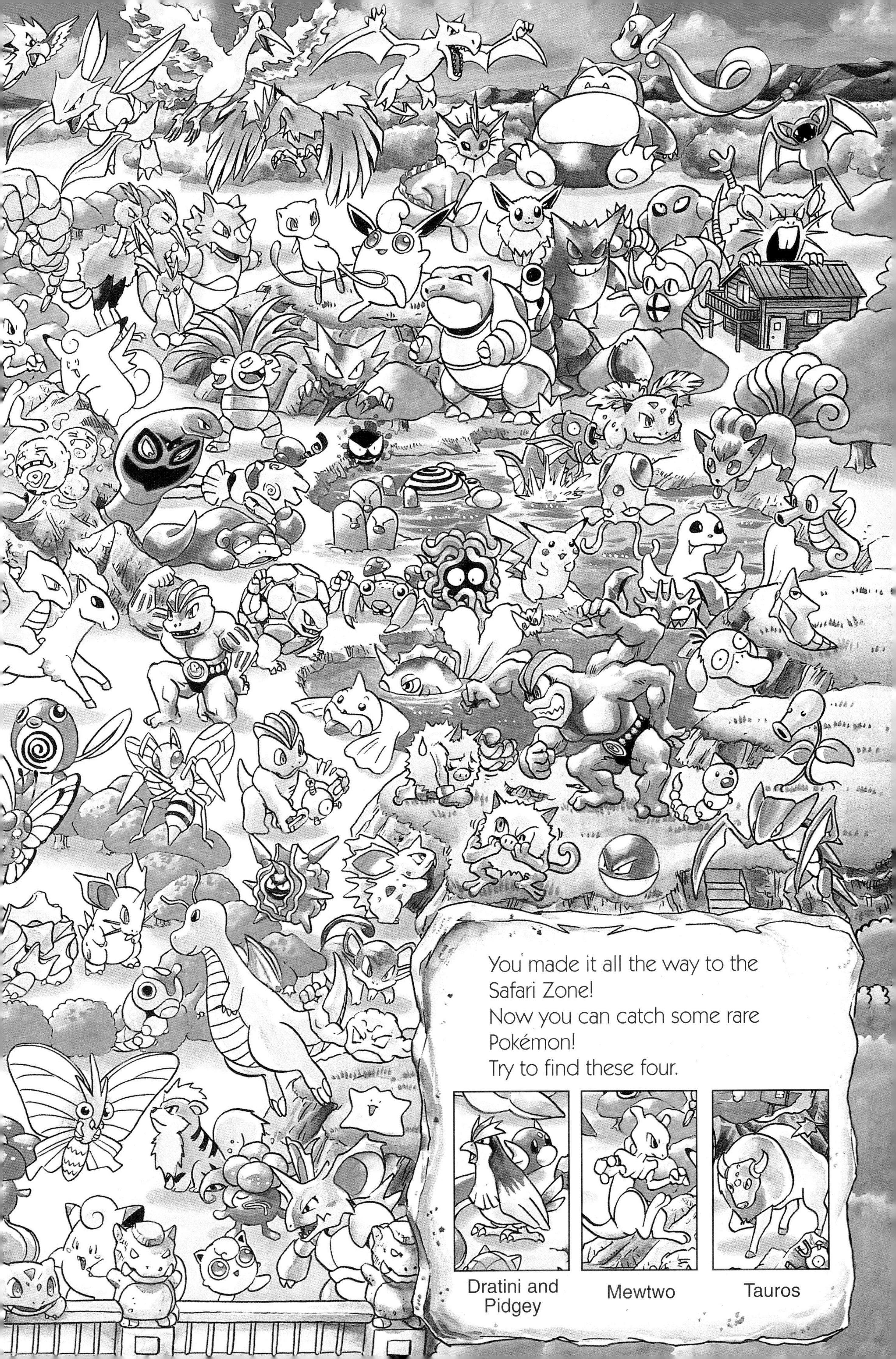

You made it all the way to the Safari Zone!
Now you can catch some rare Pokémon!
Try to find these four.

Dratini and Pidgey

Mewtwo

Tauros

THE ELITE FOUR OF INDIGO PLATEAU

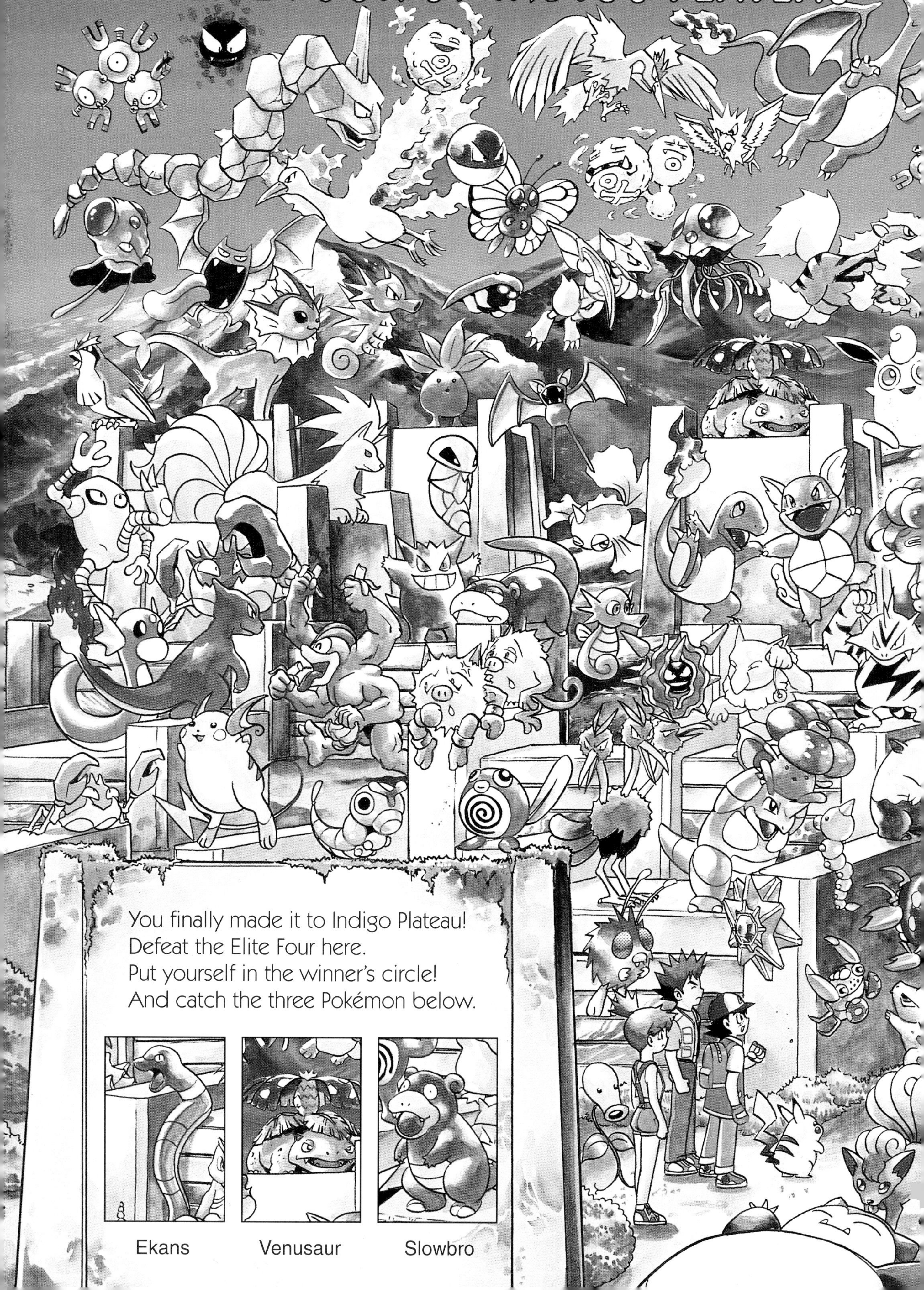
You finally made it to Indigo Plateau!
Defeat the Elite Four here.
Put yourself in the winner's circle!
And catch the three Pokémon below.
Ekans
Venusaur
Slowbro

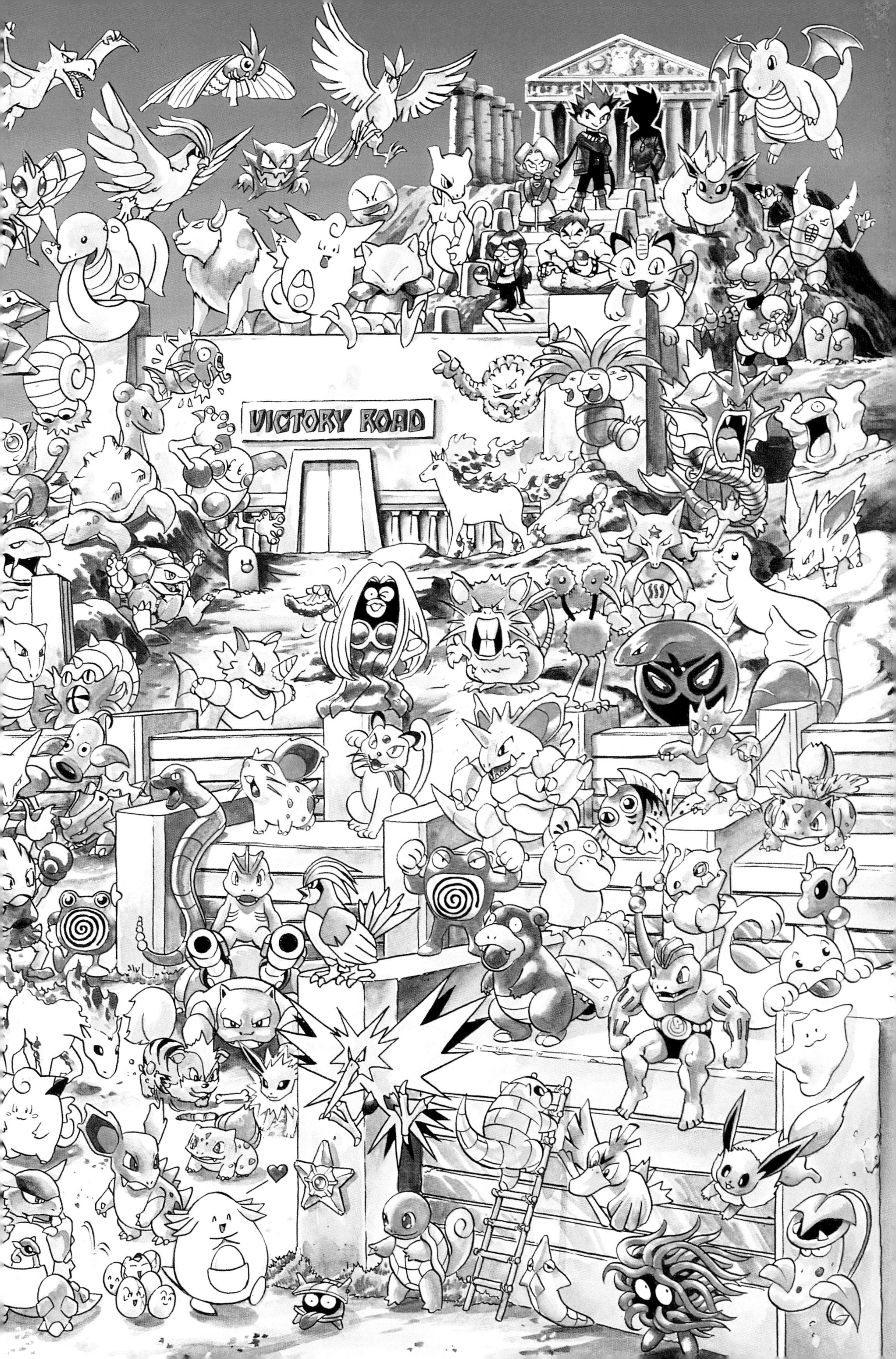
VICTORY ROAD

ANSWERS!

PALLET TOWN ON PARADE

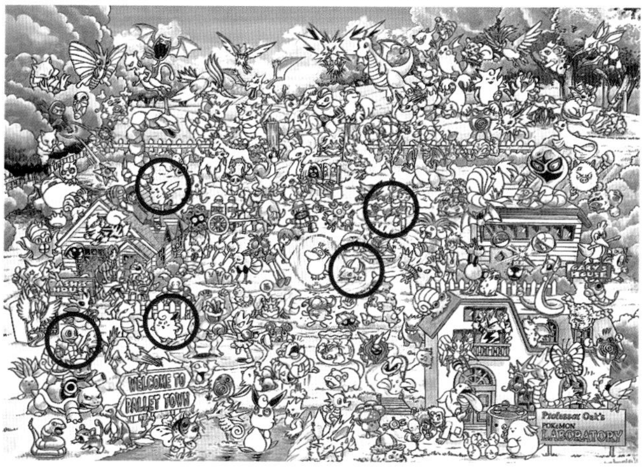
WELCOME TO PALLET TOWN
Professor Oak's POKéMON LABORATORY

LOST INSIDE MT. MOON

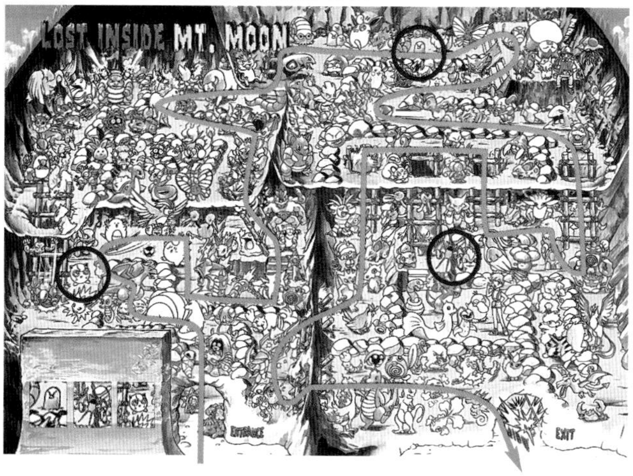
LOST INSIDE MT. MOON

THE CELADON CITY FAIR

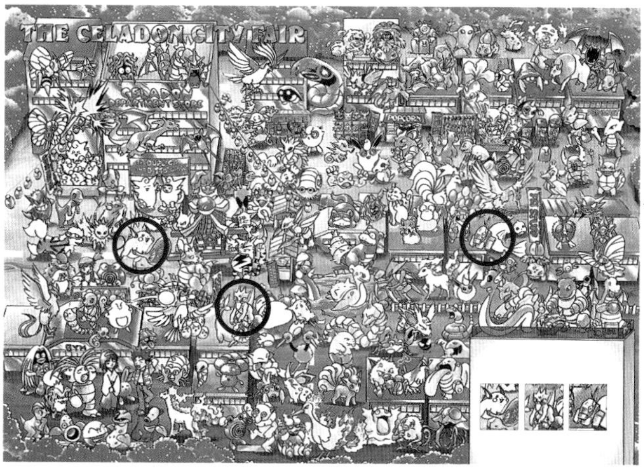
THE CELADON CITY FAIR

CATCH 'EM ALL IN THE SAFARI ZONE

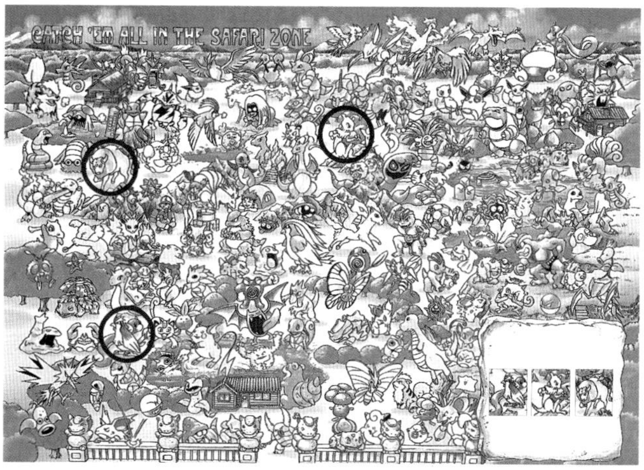
CATCH 'EM ALL IN THE SAFARI ZONE

THE A-MAZE-ING VIRIDIAN FOREST

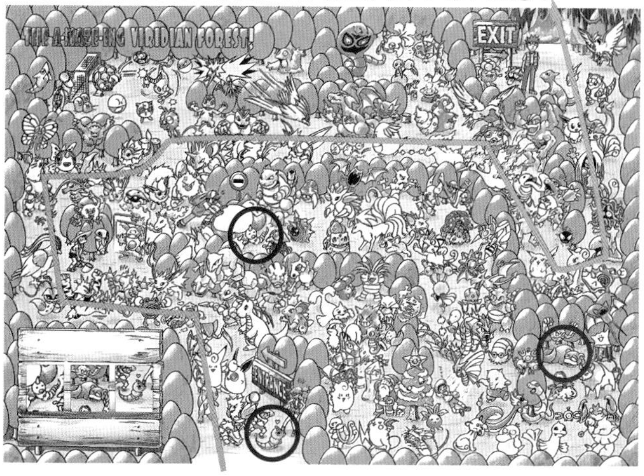
THE A-MAZE-ING VIRIDIAN FOREST!
EXIT

HIDE-AND-SEEK IN CERULEAN CITY

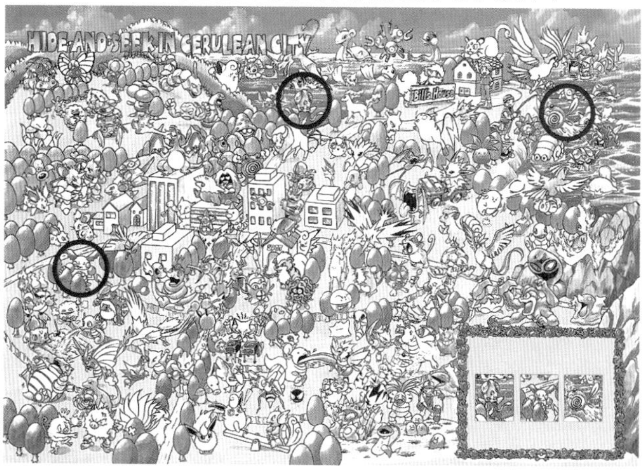
HIDE-AND-SEEK IN CERULEAN CITY

POKéMON TOWER IN LAVENDER TOWN

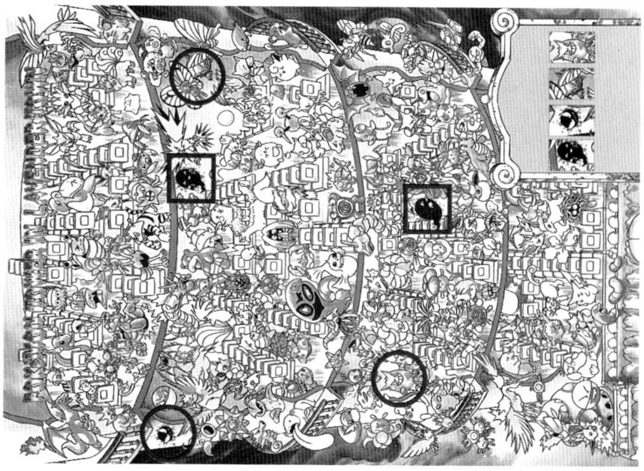

THE ELITE FOUR OF INDIGO PLATEAU

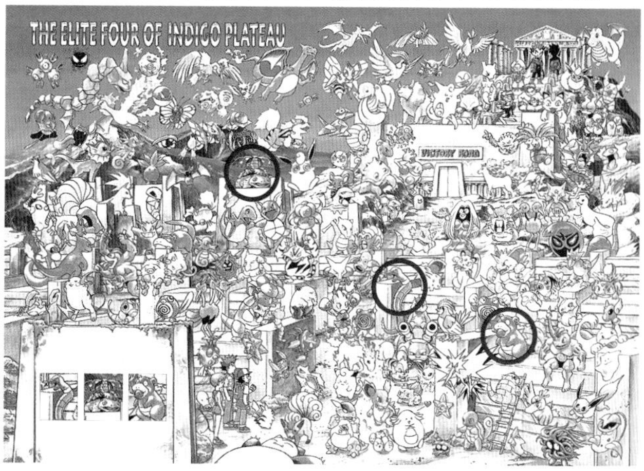
THE ELITE FOUR OF INDIGO PLATEAU

MORE DIFFICULT PUZZLES

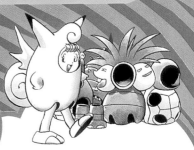

1 There is only one Mew in all the pictures in this book. Where?

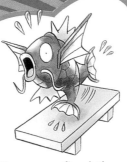

2 Can you find the Magikarp on the cutting board?

3 Duplica is pretending she is a Clefable. Can you find her?

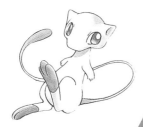

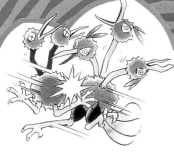

4 Where do Doduo and Dodrio crash into each other?

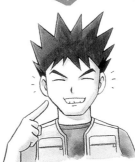

5 Brock is the gym leader of Pewter City. How many times did you see him?

6 The entire Cerulean City picture is shaped like a Pokémon. Which one?

7 Where is Machop bowling?

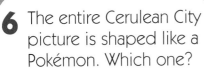

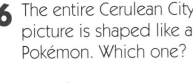

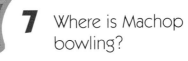

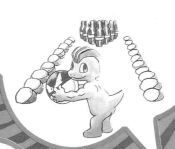

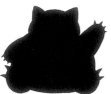

8 Not all 150 Pokémon appear in these pictures. Can you figure out which ones are missing?

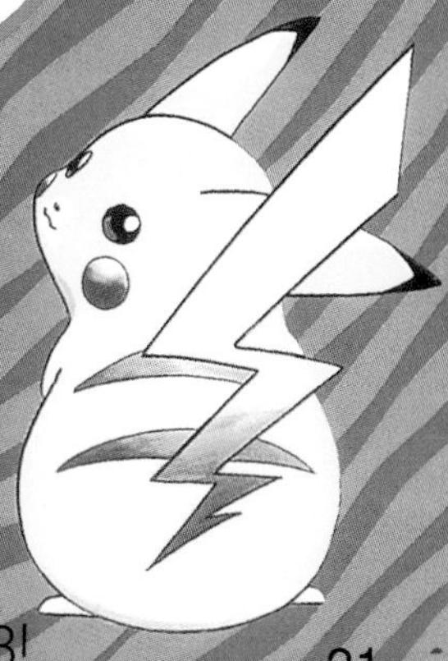

Answers on page 23!

THE MANKEY AND THE PRIMEAPE
(Where Did All the Bananas Go?)

PALLET TOWN

Mankey is swinging through the woods with its bananas. ♥

VIRIDIAN FOREST

Oh no! You'll get into trouble! You can't just throw your banana peels on the ground, Mankey!

MT. MOON

Now you did it! Primeape went and slipped on your banana peel!

CERULEAN CITY

What did you think you were doing!? Hey! Now Primeape is taking Mankey's bananas away!

CELADON CITY

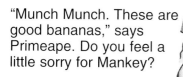

"Munch Munch. These are good bananas," says Primeape. Do you feel a little sorry for Mankey?

LAVENDER TOWN

Owch!! Look what Primeape did! Machamp has slipped on Primeape's banana peel!

SAFARI ZONE

Machamp: "Grrrrrr." Primeape: "I'm sorry, Machamp! Here, have the rest of the bananas!"

INDIGO PLATEAU

In the end, Machamp gets one banana for each of its four arms. And Mankey and Primeape cry, "No fair! Boo hoo hoo!"

EXEGGCUTE AND CHANSEY'S ADVENTURE

PALLET TOWN

Chansey discovers Exeggcute! "Huh? Are you my eggs?"

VIRIDIAN FOREST

Chansey: "Hey! Wait up!" Exeggcute: "A strange Pokémon is attacking us! Run!"

MT. MOON

Oh dear! Oh dear! Exeggcute has been carried off by Pidgeotto! Pidgeotto: "I caught my dinner!"

CERULEAN CITY

There it is! Chansey's best attack, the Egg Bomb!

CELADON CITY

Direct hit! Good aim, Chansey! (See Chansey strike a victory pose.)

LAVENDER TOWN

Pidgeotto: "Th-that hurt! Did this giant egg just hit me in the head?"

SAFARI ZONE

Pidgeotto: "Ouch! I've got a headache! I didn't really want this Exeggcute anyway! So there!"

INDIGO PLATEAU

Exeggcute: "Thank you, Chansey!" Now Chansey and Exeggcute are friends! ♥

These two stories take place in the pages of this book. Can you find each of the scenes pictured above